ARMEGEDDON IS NOT THE END

The Before, During and After Armegeddon Series of Short Stories

Stacey Wiggs

CONTENTS

FOREWORD

I don't think it would be an exaggeration to claim that an entire library could be filled with literature about futuristic events. From science fiction narratives about doomsday scenarios to the countless religious prognostications, the supply of works concerning such happenings seems to be endless. For the more scientific minded, scholarly articles and papers formulating cataclysmic calculations of how mankind might bring about their own demise are also plentiful.

By whatever media, and whether by some natural happenstance or by our own doings, the notion that this will all come to an end seems to be weighing heavily on the minds of many.

The following narratives, penned in the first person, were all written individually and compiled into the series. My goal was to make, short, engaging stories that might possibly bring a different understanding to what is going on and what is yet to happen.

I hope you enjoy, Stacey

VALHALLA

The Spartan cry the warriors code,
We hear the tales all told from old,
Of virgins fair or one's weight in gold,
The promise of Valhalla.

The call is to be your best,
to put your metal to the test,
So you can work and earn your rest,
Keep dreaming of Valhalla.

Worry not for this life,
Be the victor past the strife,
If breath be taken by the knife,
You have earned Valhalla.

When the price is laid upon the eyes,
Then truth is parted from the lies,
All too late to realize,
There is no Valhalla.

PROLOGUE

The Trip

"Grandpa, tell us a story."

"Yeah grandpa, tell us a story"

"Okay, okay. What would you like to hear?"

"The trip, tell about the trip"

"I was about twelve. My grandma Keegan had always wanted to see the ocean and that summer my dad announced it was time to take her. His business dealings were going well and he, with my mom's prompting, decided it was a good time to go.

I loved being with grandma and we spent a lot of time together. I was her "run around buddy," as she called me. Seeing how excited she was about the trip made me excited too. I told everyone I met I was going to get to see the ocean.

I don't recall much about the first part of the trip; it was just a lot of driving that I mostly slept through.

When I was not napping, grandma would point out things to me with her usual, "Would you look at that." One particular time was when we got close enough to see the mountains. I sat up in my seat to get a better look and could hardly believe what I was seeing. They rose like giants up into the clouds. A short time later we started our climb.

At one point, about half way up, dad said something about the car getting hot. A little later we stopped in a small town to check out the problem. There was a gas station there that had a repair shop on one side and and a small eatery on the other. I didn't really know what was going on, but was happy to get out and run around a little.

After the mechanic had looked the car over, he told dad it was going to take a little while to fix it. It only made sense to head next door to the diner for a bite to eat. I ordered my usual burger and fries and finished them off quickly.

When we had walked in I noticed, over in one corner, an old video game. "Space Invaders" was proudly displayed across the top and I so wanted to play. I mentioned wanting to and, much to my surprise, dad said he would play with me. He told me he had played often as a younger man while away from home on his many business ventures.

I don't know how long we played, but dad sent me several times to get more quarters. He was really good and loved showing me how to maneuver and destroy the Invaders. Our play was only cut short by the announcement the car was ready. Once assured we would have no more problems, we took off again.

I remember going up and up, so much so it seemed our ascent would never end. The clouds that had once been so far out of reach were now below us. I swear I heard both dad and the car gave a sigh of relief as we neared the summit. Once there, we stopped at a scenic overlook to give them both a break and take in the view.

Mom read a sign telling about the spot as we looked out over the surrounding forest. While they took pictures I had fun running up and down the rocks. I got as close to the edge as grandma would let me with her repeatedly telling me to be careful and get down. After soaking it all in, we started back down.

It didn't take long, after the excitement of reaching the top, for grandma and me to be fast asleep. We didn't wake until until prompted for a bathroom break and, much to our delight, we were a couple of hours closer to our destination.

For the next leg of the trip we were wide awake. We traveled though small towns and big cities with stretches of highway between them. Finally we stopped for the night as planned to give everyone a much needed rest from the ride.

The next morning, after a quick breakfast and getting checked out, we continued on. We still had a while before we would reach our destination so grandma tried her best to keep me occupied. I had never played "I spy with my little eye" before and had quite the time doing so.

Along with the game playing, I am sure my parents got tired of me asking if we were there yet. I was surprised they never scolded me for asking. Finally my mom said; "Do you smell that? That is ocean air."

It was more than I could have imagined and I don't know who was the bigger kid, me or grandma. We splashed in the water, built sand castles and bask in the warm sunshine. Often times though we would just stand and look out over the water.

Its vastness was hard to comprehend. We made a game of seeing who could spot a boat out the farthest, a game my younger eyes gave me an advantage in playing.

The last day of our stay, as we looked out for the final time, she said to me; "Just think about it, somewhere over the water is another little boy and his grandma looking back at us."

I was so glad we were able to go and see it together.

AFTER 999

Volume IV

I was born after. Eleven generations of Keegans have come before me and I, like my ancestors, must bring our bounty to the great city. The city we are not allowed to enter.

I have heard the stories of the time before, the time when mankind was on the verge of its crowning achievement. The time of unity and peace that brought great prosperity to all who would join in. The time when most walked as one under the guidance of the greatest leader mankind had ever known. Under his supreme leadership most rulers of the prospective regions had rallied to his cause.

It is told there were some who could not see the vision of our great leader and criticized his every achievement toward worldwide unification.

Eventually preparations had to be made to finally rid the land of the scourge of those remaining religious zealots.

The armies of the individual regions were incorporated for the crusade to cleanse mother earth of this resistance. This action would undoubtedly bring about the glorious new age with all its majesty. As the buildup and deployment took shape, the image of what we could achieve together would be on the brink of fulfillment. I am told shouts of joy echoed throughout the land as the final assault was made.

It was then the Invaders came. Of what they were and from where they came, I do not know. The stories of that time claim many of their kind had infiltrated our world long ago. As it is told, just prior to their invasion, the infiltrators were reunited with the Invaders in order to increase their forces.

It was not just their sheer numbers that changed the outcome of the purification, the Invaders' weaponry was like none the world had ever seen. Sadly, the battle was a complete loss for our glorious leader and the rulers who followed him. I know of none that survived.

After the loss, those of this world who were not killed were forced to bow to the Invaders' victorious king and serve under his rule. It has been that way ever since. Concerning the Infiltrators, they are now our overseers.

I have also heard of what the earth was before. Of numerous mountains that reached toward the sky and masses of water that surrounded the separated lands.

It would seem the power of the Invaders was not limited to their weapons. During their offensive the terrain as it was then was reformed to their liking. The only high ground now remaining is that of their great city.

I must admit the city's walls are an amazing thing to behold as they can be seen from a great distance. Their foundations shine like jewels and their gates are as giant pearls. The glow that comes from within can be seen before the walls even come into view. One can barely comprehend all of their vastness and beauty. It makes one wonder what may be seen within their boundaries.

So once again, I travel as instructed to their city. To bring what the overseers call our offering to them. As always, I will leave my family's portion at one of the gates as I will not be allowed in. So it has been for the leaders of my clan who came before and thus it is for me.

At first it is just myself and those whom I lead that travel together, but as the journey continues the caravan grows. Others, who are also making their way, join in at every junction along the route.

The solemn procession usually continues along

with mostly mild pleasantries being exchanged. Even among those of us who have traveled together before the chatter is usually limited. What is there to talk about? This is something we must do.

However, this year's pilgrimage is starting to take on an unusual turn. With each additional family joining in, the more discussion I hear.

One of the topics being passed around, by some who have joined in, is the claim our glorious leader from the time past was of the same as the Invaders. They are also insisting he was not killed as many thought, only exiled for a time. Others tell that he is no longer banished from the land and is making plans to lead us to take back what is rightfully ours.

As the days pass and our numbers grow there is more and more talk. Some of the latest entrants are even claiming to have seen him and received his words, but I still remain unconvinced.

I try not to be skeptical, but I have heard such stories before and they always amounted to nothing. There is still too much travel required to get overly involved in what may only be gossip.

BEFORE 1.0

Volume I

There is only one way for me to describe it, the New Dark Ages. It is not as in previous times, when information was withheld in order to control the narrative, but a massive dump of information that has ultimately overloaded the rational thinking processes of many. More material can be accessed about any subject matter imaginable than ever before. Countless 'experts', with convoluted trains of logic that would leave even the most astute scratching their heads, drone on and on about every topic possible.

Much like the prior Dark Ages, when people's emotions where used as a tool to override logic, the New Dark Ages utilizes the same tactic. The airways are replete with commercials that tug on one's heartstrings in order to elicit a compassionate response to their perspective agendas. To the contrary, the news outlets, in order to gain viewership, place the emphasis on promoting a more visceral reaction. Emotions are being tugged to and fro intentionally on a daily basis.

Now it is not just relegated to the secular world; the religious factions are guilty of much the same. Offers for countless books, videos and study materials, promoted by their prospective authors, flood religious media. Often within these works a single phrase is extrapolated to the utmost reaches of sensibility.

Simple concepts are relegated to the status of unworthy of one's time while "secret codes" and the like gain in popularity. Needless to say the religious community has been fragmented into numerous sects each vying for the greatest following of their perspective doctrines.

The end result of the overload of information and emotions is a world that is aware of everything but understands nothing about what is really going on.

BEFORE 2.0

Our convoy grew as we traveled toward the capital. We thought surely they will have to hear us because of our vast numbers. To try and prevent any misunderstandings of our intent, every effort was made to ensure all involved parties knew our agenda was totally peaceable.

Our progression was going smoothly and everyone seemed to be in good spirits. That was before we encountered the unthinkable.

Some miles out, and without warning, almost the entirety of our motorcade was stopped in its tracks. The only remaining vehicles with the ability to move forward were those so antiquated they operated without the aid of onboard computers. (I must say many of us laughed as they joined in, but we now see the folly of our mocking.)

The modern technology, which had enhanced our lives in so many ways, was now being used against us.

Even if we could have gathered those few stalwart machines, of simpler technology that could still function, to try and move a select group forward, the gridlock of the incapacitated blocked our advancement.

The realization that we might not achieve our agenda left many feeling frustrated and it was shocking how quickly chaos ensued.

Our leaders tried to maintain order, but our numbers quickly fragmented. The enraged took off toward our objective on foot while the disillusioned turned away in like manner.

Most disheartening was that most were simply too preoccupied with trying to get their now disabled transportation back to functioning to gather a usable crowd.

I am afraid to even think of how the media is going to spin this and what repercussions we will all face in the coming days.

BEFORE 2.7

Volume V

I had been searching for a place to belong for quite some time. Be it a civic or religious organization, it just always seemed I didn't fit in. I am sure you know how that feels. I had lost count of how many meetings I had attended. No matter the affiliation, or how hard I tried, sooner or later something would always let me know I did not belong.

A friend told me he knew of a group that was very different from the others I had tried. He added, from what he knew about me, it would be more to my liking.

He said they met at the old VFW hall just outside of town and that he could let me know when to attend. After a little more discussion, I decided to give fitting in one more shot.

As I approached the main entrance a sign directed all to use the side door. I followed a paved path around the building and made my way in. I found myself in a short hall with painted block walls and tile floors. This was not uncommon at the time as it made for durable construction and easy cleaning. Two doors, evenly spaced and clearly marked as restrooms, lined one side. The remaining interior door stood opposite at the far end with no markings. A sign occupied the wall in one's line of sight when entering, but I paid it little mind and went straight to the unmarked door. It was locked.

I stepped back to see if directions for entry were given on the sign.

At the top it said "Read this out loud". I chuckled at the idea but said to myself "what the heck" and then did as instructed.

When I started on the first lines it was more of a mumble than a reading out loud.

"I am a Christian Anarchist.
I hold dear the authority of only one king, the Son of the Most High,"

I suddenly found myself frozen in time as my mind went back many years. I was raised in the country and attended a small rural high school. Like many of that time and place, I took agricultural management classes as one of my electives. Suddenly the creed we recited for the associated organization came flooding back to my mind.

I regained my composure and restarted the reading

with the same gusto we were prompted to use those many years ago.

"I am a Christian Anarchist.
I hold dear the authority of only one king, the Son of the Most High, authority granted to Him by the Father.
I believe if I follow Him no man has any true authority over me.
No king, no priest, no soldier, no perpetrator of good or evil, or any lifted up by man, through threat of violence or coercion, be it physical or otherwise, controls my destiny."

As I proceeded I could not help but notice as my words reverberated in the confined space. The hardened surfaces promoted a most intense ring with the effect often giving me a slight chill. As I continued my voice grew more powerful with each word recited.

"I do not advocate violence or seek chaos; I strive to live at peace with all.
I believe in free trade with those who also embrace this perfect concept.
My acquiescence to the rules of man is not recognition of their presumed authority, but a submitting to the authority of the Most High and to His Word.
No decree of man will hold sway under the judgment of the Lord and I shall fear Him who created all and not the created."

When I finished my narration I was so enraptured in

the moment I barely perceived the slight click of the door being unlocked. It was then I knew I had found my place.

BEFORE 3.1

My beloved,

I am sorry once again that I am unable to be there with you and the girls. I hope this day goes much better for you and the pause in treatments you have been receiving permit for a few days of rest before the move begins.

As we have talked, the narrative is peace, but I feel with most urgency that staying within the annexation is not in our best interest. Many others feel the same but also feel duty-bound to remain, no matter the tribulations.

All is in place for our relocation. The movers have their instructions as to your limitations and I feel confident it will be of little stress. My mother will be there to take care of the girls and any incidentals that might arise.

The new housing may not be all we had prayed for. However, it will allow me to spend more time with you and the girls, as opposed to the occasional weekend visit.

It is also very close to the medical services needed for your continued treatments. I know the travels to and from the center have taken a toll on you and the doctors agree that being nearby will be beneficial.

The best of news is my recent promotion that allows for this all to be possible. The pay raise with the allowance for off-base housing is surely a blessing from YHWH and could not have come at a better time.

I so look forward to being able to see your smile.
All my love,
Aviel

BEFORE 4.2

We thought we were properly prepared and, by any logical means of assessment, it would have been difficult for anyone to have done better. An isolated location, ample food stocks, fresh water supply and storage, required tools and equipment, reinforced buildings and cellars, local game and the capacity to resupply our garden stuffs with heritage seeds and plants (not to mention arms and ammunition) made for an ideal survival situation.

What we were not prepared for was the physiological toil the responsibility and isolation would take upon many of the group.

At first it was just a few random complaints, like wanting a particular order from a favorite restaurant chain or the longing for nicer accommodations. As the months passed, the complaints morphed into full on outbursts of discontent. I guess in hindsight we had all fallen for the apocalyptic doomsayer's predictions of a ravaged earth. When it did not happen as anticipated things started to unravel.

During the readiness phase economic commitments were made by all. What I would discover later is that not everyone was as dedicated as they had let on to be. I now know that many had held on to certain assets and kept them in secret outside our facility.

Further into our stay, without the world economy collapsing as we thought, it was easy to see who had not gone all in with our project. This being confirmed when they packed a few things and left.

Others found reasons to be gone for longer and longer periods of time until they simply did not return. I suppose they were making accommodations elsewhere while away from the camp.

Then word was brought in that financial assistance was available just for the asking to anyone willing to rejoin society. It didn't take long for our numbers to decrease to the point where the fullness of our intentions no longer had the manpower to be sustainable.

Sadly, much of what we have built will inevitably fall into disrepair and production will be limited without the man-hours we once had available for such tasks.

On the bright side, those few of us that remain will have no problem with wanting for the basics. There are more than enough long-term supplies for an extended stay for the smaller number still here.

I hope the resolve of those of us who remain will take us through even with this less than ideal situation.

I guess I really shouldn't judge to harshly those who have fallen short of our intentions, because a fresh, hot meat-lovers pizza sure does sound good about now.

BEFORE 5.6

Volume VI

Before we go any farther; Yes! The anti, the denier, the mandate resister or any others who can't see how the greater good is being served, all get what they deserve. They have had enough time to comply; it didn't have to come to this.

Of them all, the Avoiders, the ones that somehow thought by some miraculous means they would not have to conform to the recognized new world dictates, are the most emotionally exhausting to deal with. They cry, they beg, they fall to their knees, and often I do feel for them, but ultimately I must do my duty. In the end most just stand there with dejected looks on their faces as I carry out my orders.

At first this was all quite easy. For most the thought of losing their life's savings, retirement or current income was more than enough to gain compliance, but as time has passed and the resisters have gotten fewer my job has gotten tougher. These last holdouts simply don't seem to have the capacity to comprehend it is all for the greater good.

For the life of me, I just don't understand. With unilateral peace, guaranteed housing, paid utilities and a life that most could only dream of before the great alliance, why would anyone not want to be part of this new world and all it has to offer?

BEFORE 5.9

My Dear Friend,

I hope this letter finds you well and in good spirits. I know my forced absence was abrupt, but we both know it was not totally unexpected. At least I am being allowed some contact at this point.

I have been unofficially named a contrarian and, I must admit, it is somewhat true as I do often oppose popular opinion. As you know, when I do, I do not oppose such things without due consideration and have devoted much study to assure the accuracy of my statements.

I am sure some who do not know me well may think my current incarceration stems from some militant political stance against the government or the unlawful avoidance of taxation. However, both of those have been proven untrue. One in my position can never know what is being touted publicly though.

As it stands at present, the official reason for my continued confinement is the only remaining claim of "Sedition against the Holy Universal Church."

You had warned me and I knew this day might come eventually, but in my naivety I never thought it would come so soon and from someone so close (a mistake I will not make again if ever freed). To that point, I am not sure if this letter will even find you as I know your safeguards are much more stringent than my own.

I know this is a big favor to ask, but if there is anyone willing to provide a counter to the claim of sedition, I would appreciate their assistance so this matter might be settled sooner than later.

Your Friend in Chains

BEFORE 6.0

Volume VIII

I was born a preacher's daughter. My mother told me the only way to keep me from crying, as an infant during my dad's preaching, was to place me in my carrier on the platform near his pulpit.

As I grew and was able to sit on my own I graduated to the mourner's bench. I never sat in the pews with the rest of the congregation. Often times, to my dad's delight, other children would join me on my perch, not to mention the repentant.

His voice would frequently boom like thunder during his sermons, but was always as gentle as a dove with me and anyone else that made their way to the mourner's bench. It was his overwhelming passion coupled with his kindness that made me never doubt his words.

That is why I am struggling now. He always told us the devout would be spared the troubles of the worldly and I have always adhered to that promise.

It started a few years ago with a few being labeled as intolerant and guilty of hate speech. In time it progressed to entire assemblies being shut down. Bank accounts were frozen, properties seized and leaders jailed for, as the perpetrators call it, non-compliance to the "universally accepted truths." Once jailed, many are never seen or heard from again.

Now it is not simply the keeping of my faith that presses me, but the struggles to even survive apart from the world governmental system. During the last few months compliance has become mandatory and enforcement is spreading to all levels of civilization. Many institutions will no longer even do business unless a person has a high enough, what they have deemed, social credit score and the insignia to prove its validity.

I surely wish my dad was here now to guide me, as I am not sure I can endure.

BEFORE 6.2

There they are again, the last devoted few, gathered together on the steps of their once packed sanctified place. The parking lot that was often beyond capacity can now handle the stragglers easily. There used to be thousands that showed up and oh the celebrations they had.

I remember when I was very young the first time I got talked into going. There was singing, loud music, flashing lights, people jumping up and down. It was quite the spectacle to see. I attended a few times but bored when I figured out that was their regular routine. I preferred to run the streets instead as there was always something new going on.

Now I would make sure to go when they held special events. One time, believe it or not, they set up a bicycle stunt show complete with ramps and jumps. For a poor kid growing up in the city; it was like being able to go to the circus. We lived close by, so it was no skin off my nose to get some free entertainment. Also, during their "feasts" as they called them, I would go just to get a delicious meal. Some of those ladies could really cook. They always professed an open door policy, even for those of us who did not attend their regular services, so why not take advantage?

Now the doors are chained and the lot barricaded. I don't see any big meals or free entertainment going on, but some do still make their way back in every week, even though I have heard they have been told not to.

"Are we leaving today? Should I pack my bags?" I know they hear my shouts but they never answer back. They claimed they weren't going to be here now and were going to be swept away to nirvana or something like that. I told one of them the best way to nirvana was a couple of pain pills, a muscle relaxer, a shot of booze and maybe a joint or two just in case. He was not amused.

They kept coming around until finally I had had enough and really ripped into them about their cult. They stopped talking to me after that.

Oh well, that is enough entertainment for the day. Maybe I'll see how much is left on my EBT card and go trade some groceries for a trip to nirvana.

DURING 6.8

Volume I

I must say, as a logistics officer for the Consolidated Armies, being on duty during the buildup and deployment has been exhausting while also being tremendously satisfying. I am proud to have been involved. The amount of cooperation that has been required to mobilize such a force is almost beyond imagination, but thankfully, not beyond our ability.

Our achievement is not simply the chain of command doing its duty, but the unparalleled guidance that has come down from, one can arguably say, mankind's greatest leader. As a student of military history I feel safe in saying he has brought innovative methods and usage to battlefield preparation and siege strategy.

Natural obstacles have been overcome with amazing

swiftness and will allow for a continuous flow of soldiers, armaments and all supporting services. Simultaneous land, air and marine assaults have been coordinated to the finest detail and with precise timing.

The campaign should only last days, if not hours. Our casualties are expected to be light, as all contingencies have been accounted for and the ability of the resistance pales in comparison to our unified forces.

Now we wait for what will surely be a great victory.

DURING 6.9

Volume II

Dear Mother,

I was so relieved to finally receive word from you that you and the girls had reached your destination safely. I know this whole ordeal has been a struggle since the passing of their mother, but as father would have said; "Family, family is what is important." Knowing mine is out of harm's way gives me the strength to carry on.

As you have always instructed, I pray daily that the miracle will happen and our great land will be spared, but it grows harder each hour as the masses advance more toward our beloved city.

I have been called, I must go.
Aviel

DURING 6.9.9

There is nothing better to be doing during a time like this than to be sitting at my favorite pub. The multiple screens around the room give a real time display as the events of the unification unfold. The final holdouts are about to be brought into submission.

The barkeep provides a steady flow as we all cheer our favorite forces on. Lou, a retired Marine, scoffs at Bill, the "fly-boy" as he calls him, as Bill tells of the superiority of an airborne attack. Pete counters with how much pounding a well-equipped naval assault can provide. Eugene, (not his real name but one penned to him after a character from a popular TV show) our local self-proclaimed military expert, even though he has never served, chimes in that all must work together,. The banter is all in good fun as we each share the pride of our perspective branches.

Our eyes stay affixed to the broadcasts as the battle plan plays out. Our rivalry diminishes as we watch all fall into place. Despite our individual affiliations, we all agree this is the greatest military campaign ever conceived.

Silence fills the bar as we are caught off guard by the sudden flash from the screens and the now total blankness that is displayed about the room. What is going on?

DURING 7.0

Volume IV

The last few moments have changed everything here in the war room. Initially all was going per plan and it was unthinkable that anything other than light resistance would be met.

"Private, stop screaming into the transmitter."
"But Sir, I have lost B Company!"
"I Know son, calm down and keep trying."

It is the same scenario down the line as several companies of soldiers have lost contact. My counterparts are confirming multiple aircraft destroyed and the last report was that most of the marine division had been decimated.

Everyone is scrambling for answers. How could this have happened?

AFTER 001.0

Volume I

Much like the Jimmy Buffet song, I can't say it was any body's fault but my own. I attended services, gave when the plate was passed, got semi-involved with projects, but for the most part, just attended out of a sense of obligation and to insure my status amongst my peers.

I did listen at times, but only when it suited me. Now when I could hold a teaching over someone's head I could certainly recount a lesson. Other than that, one would have been hard pressed to get much out of me on any subject. One could say, I was neither hot nor cold.

I also cannot blame others for their lack of trying to get me more involved. I was just too busy living my life to be bothered by what I thought was just attention-getting nonsense on their part.

I know I was not alone as myself and others would often refer to those who pressed the matter as eccentric or, at times, a more derogatory term.

I really thought I had it all figured out and would not be in this situation. To my defence, there were plenty of others who claimed there was nothing to worry about. They assured me my financial support of their organization would be more than adequate for my inclusion.

However, here I sit, having watched the events unfold, wishing I would not have scoffed at those who were sounding the warning.

AFTER 018.4

Volume II

I guess one really should not laugh about it, but it is too funny not to. You see, I know I got what was coming to me as us Keegans have always been a notorious lot.

I played my part in the business world for all to see. If you had dealings with me you knew to be on your guard. Your item was always junk and mine was made of gold. What I would offer someone when buying and what I would ask for that same item when selling was always miles apart. I would also always make sure to have a story about why it was so. Most knew how to deal with me and would haggle me down to a reasonable price, but for those unsuspecting few, great gain was mine for the taking.

Now there were also those in our town who were

touted as honest men. You know the ones, the profitable property owner, the banker, the local government worker, all those whose lofty positions were held in high esteem within the community. They sat on church councils, served as deacons in congregations and were appointed to every civic position out there.

From the local school board to the various city or the county offices, being part of their clique insured no one would dare question their actions. Knowing that any attempt to expose their transgressions might result in one's own harm, most everyone sought to be in their good favor. As a result, their ethics were seldom challenged.

Now to the funny part, we had all heard about the coming and were present when it happened. Some of us knew we had no chance and were resolved to face our fate, but then there were those I spoke of.

They just knew they were going to be part of it. They presumed they were the standard by which others would be judged. They never had their business practices brought into question or their name slandered at the local gas station. They were above reproach, or so it seemed.

Now here we all are, with them still looking for answers and wondering why this has happened to them.

So forgive me if I chuckle a little as I am sure they never imagined their lot would be thrown in with mine.

AFTER 308.1

Volume III

I am the third generation of the Keegan family to be born after. The stories, handed down from my great grandparents, who lived through and witnessed the events, still bear witness to us of those days. As it is told, things did not happen as many of that time claimed they would.

There was no third Great War or natural pestilence that wiped out most living in those days. No mass bombings of individual nations into nonexistence. No asteroids raining down fire destroying our atmosphere. No earthquakes and their resulting tsunamis wiping out entire populations.

Quite the contrary, for most all was harmony and the taming of nature suited food production like never before. It was a wondrous time I am told.

That is not to say all lived in peace or enjoyed a

prosperous life, but, from what I hear, the struggle of mankind to survive had been all but done away with.

As the story goes, there was one who had risen among the elite who was leading this new age of enlightenment and its resulting prosperity. By him peace was brought too many regions that for centuries had known only conflict.

Alliances were forged between rival nations bringing an end to most economic struggles and to all but a few religious divisions. Nations that once coveted their individual money values were brought together under one unified currency. This allowed for all who would join a level playing field and equal advantage.

He was touted as the greatest leader of all time even before the revelation was publicized that he had descended from a royal linage. This came to light only after the Holy Church had opened its archives for greater examination. Upon investigation, research seemed to prove what had been alleged for decades and there was a living, rightful heir.

There had been speculation that the once thought savior was not the last beneficiary of the royal line. That it had been the duty of a devote few to protect the revealing of that linage until the appointed time.

Apparently it was more than speculation and that time had come at last. The great leader's pedigree was confirmed by the Pontiff and he was then allowed to stand where no one had before for the entire world to see.

This new announcement. coupled with his accomplishments on behalf of mankind, cemented his status and most acknowledged him as supreme.

His only remaining desire was to rid the earth of the last holdouts that opposed his rule and bring the whole world into unity.

Little did he or anyone else know, the cosmos had other plans.

GRANDPA'S STORY

Our Family

"I met your grandmother while running a sales route and we dated each other off and on for several years. We both had plans for our lives and our careers and that did not include any overly strenuous personal attachments. It was not uncommon in those days for many to wait until they were in their thirties to make the commitment of marriage.

Eventually, but only after we knew our perspective finances were secure and we had lived enough of our lives independently, we did marry.

After settling into our new life together, we discussed the topic of when to start a family. Much consideration was given to the topic and we came to the only logical decision. With all the talk of natural and man-made disasters looming on the horizon, bringing a child into such a troubled world would not be fair to them. We were both healthy and knew of many that waited well into their forties to start a family, so we knew we still had plenty of time.

Or patience to wait paid off when the revelation came that our doomed planet had been given a fresh hope of survival. A new leader had risen and was at last bringing peace and prosperity throughout much of the world. Old ways of thinking were in the process of completely being erased from the narrative.

His new and innovative ideas were facilitating fulfillment of the progressive movement's agenda faster than ever before. Life at its fullest was available to all for just a quick agreement and a slight prick of the skin.

There were still some who tried to hang onto their old ways, but they were fewer and fewer as the days progressed. With total world peace just a short time away, it was then time to start a family.

We had no idea of what all would take place during the next few months. If we had, I am sure none of you Keegans would be here. I am so happy we did not know."

GRANDMA KEEGAN'S LETTER

My Dear Sweet Baby Boy,

The last few months awaiting your arrival have been challenging to say the least. Who would have thought the world that existed at your conception would have changed so much by the time of your birth. One cannot say it is not beautiful, it is just so different.

Your father and I waited many years before starting a family. He tells it was a mutual decision, but in reality it was his choice, like most things for us were.

I met him while I was attending college and I must admit I was instantly smitten. His athletic build and extroverted manner were enough to attract many, but it was when he smiled at me that I was forever lost. From that point on I would follow his lead for our lives. When he announced it was time to pursue being parents, I was more than overjoyed.

The world had been at peace for a quite some time, but how quickly that would change. Even when things started to unfold they seemed far away. Your father assured me what was going on was for the greater good and not to worry.

For many years, when younger, I had tried to make sense of it all for myself. Your father never shared in my concern and often rebuffed me for wasting my time. I must admit, after hearing his many conflicting arguments about the subject, I simply fell away from trying to understand.

We did have a good life and I was happy to be finally starting a new chapter that would include you.

It was a gorgeous fall day and we were relieved to have some time off to explore the countryside. For those next few hours it was nice to shut the rest of the world out of our lives. No work, no breaking news, just us and the new life I carried.

The clouds added to our tranquility as we

traveled though the many farms along our route. I had packed a picnic lunch for us and we found the perfect spot to enjoy it. All was at peace.

At first it was just a slight rumbling of the ground that your father assured me would pass. However, it did not, it only grew stronger. As the rumbling continued, the sky took on a most intense brightness, to the point, as the clouds began to move apart, the sun appeared only as a black dot.

Even though it was at quite some distance from us, there was no way not to witness the event. As it drew nearer to the ground the earth began to quake most violently. The shaking ultimately brought us both to our knees. As I knelt there in fear, with my arms wrapped firmly around you, I confessed all we had achieved in this world could have been in vain.

After some time, when the quaking had finally subsided, I found the strength to stop crying and open my eyes. Your father had already managed to make it to his feet and was shouting for me to come and look.

Off in the distance we could see great billows of smoke ascending upward for what seemed like forever. We could only imagine what was taking place.

As we made our way back in we would learn that many cities, including our own, had been reduced to rubble. Our plan for a perfect day had been shattered.

With the nexus of our wealth now being desolate, we could not help but mourn and wonder how we would survive.

AFTER 999C

Much to my delight the rumors have proven to be true and I stand corrected. Our glorious leader does live. I did not trust the reports until I finally got to see him and hear him speak for myself.

After hearing him in person, it is easy to see why everyone is rallying to his cause. His words are unlike any other and are an inspiration for those of us wishing to escape this tyranny.

He calls us to rid ourselves of this new scourge and restore mankind's rightful kingdom. His confidence in it happening, coupled with his relentless pursuit to bring the whole earth together once again, is truly motivational.

The very prospect of not having to bow down and

give up what is mine to those Invaders is almost more than I can hope for. I am proud to be a called to be part of such a historic event. I can hardly wait.

In years past there has not been this great of number traveling our route toward their city at once. The line goes on as far as I can see in front and behind me. We all assume that is part of the plan.

I am sure others, like myself, are wanting to sound off and start our charge. However, for now we are supposed to continue or journey at the regular pace and hold our tongues as not to alert our oppressors. To be covertly ready for battle, but appear as subtle as always, is a solid strategy.

As we grow closer and the walls come into view our formation is joined by others coming from all directions. As we press on we form a vast multitude ready to take back what is ours. I am confident of our triumph. We just have to wait a little longer.

"Be patient my brothers and sisters, it won't be long now."

Finally we are all gathered and the order is given. The masses start their move forward as a collective. Each individual now fortified with the realization that our longing for this day has come to fruition. Their city will surely fall.

"Onward to our rightful destiny!"

Our triumph is shouted as we move hastily toward

our prize.

The front most part of the multitude charges nearer the walls with the sure strength of will. When allowed by the surge I, along with the others I lead, begin our advance. We all want to play our part. We press inward with confidence.

"Stop! Something is wrong. Stop! Stop!"

I hear the words as they make their way back toward my family and I raise myself up to see what is happening. To my dread, I watch as those nearest the wall begin to be consumed with fire. As the blaze intensifies the cries of the forward fill the air and pierce the ears.

The soon to be engulfed attempt to turn in retreat, but it is of no avail. The sheer numbers packed together prevent any withdrawal. Surely we will all be overtaken by the flame.

I am afraid.

EPILOGUE

*And I saw an angel come down from
heaven, having the key of the bottomless
pit and a great chain in his hand.*

*And he laid hold on the dragon, that old
serpent, which is the Devil, and Satan,
and bound him a thousand years,*

*And cast him into the bottomless pit, and
shut him up, and set a seal upon him, that he
should deceive the nations no more, till the
thousand years should be fulfilled: and after
that he must be loosed a little season…….*

*And when the thousand years are expired,
Satan shall be loosed out of his prison,*

*And shall go out to deceive the nations which
are in the four quarters of the earth, Gog, and
Magog, to gather them together to battle: the
number of whom is as the sand of the sea.*

*And they went up on the breadth of the earth,
and compassed the camp of the saints about,
and the beloved city: and fire came down from
God out of heaven, and devoured them.*